S is for Snowman

God's Wintertime Alphabet

By Kathy-jo Wargin

Illustrated by Richard Johnson

ZONDERkidz

ZONDERVAN.com/
AUTHORTRACKER
follow your favorite authors

ZONDERKIDZ

S Is for Snowman
Copyright © 2011 by Kathy-jo Wargin
Illustrations copyright © 2011 by Richard G. Johnson

Requests for information should be addressed to:
Zonderkidz, Grand Rapids, Michigan 49530

Library of Congress Cataloging-in-Publication Data

Wargin, Kathy-jo.
　　　S is for snowman / written by Kathy-jo Wargin.
　　　p. cm.
　　　Summary: Presents rhyming sentences for each letter of the alphabet that remind the reader of God's blessings in winter.
　　　ISBN 978-0-310-71661-7 (hardcover)
　　　[1. Stories in rhyme. 2. Winter—Fiction. 3. God—Fiction. 4. Alphabet.] I. Title.
PZ8.3.W2172Saai 2011
[E]—dc22
2009037507

Editor: Barbara Herndon
Art direction: Jody Langley

Printed in China

11 12 13 14 15 16 /LPC/ 10 9 8 7 6 5 4 3 2 1

To Jake and Ed, for the warmth and laughter you bring to every season.
K.W.

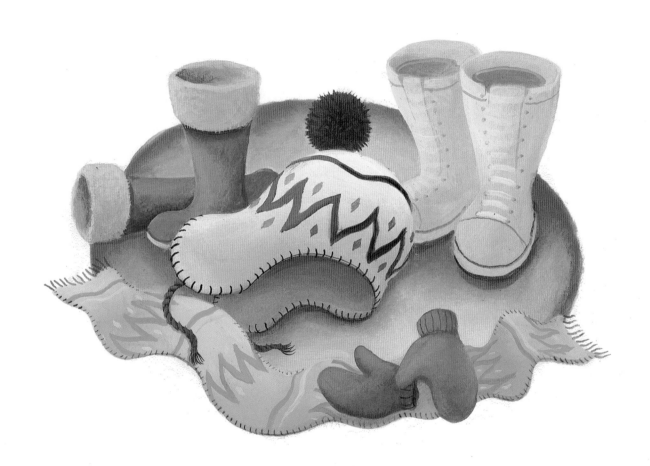

For Sushila
Love, Richard

A is for Angels

White snowy **A**ngels with wide sweeping wings—
let's find the wonders that God's winter brings.

B is for Birds

Winter brings **B**irds busy searching for seed.
We'll fill the feeders to give what they need.

C is for Cookies

We can bake Cookies to eat and to share
and bring them to neighbors to show that we care.

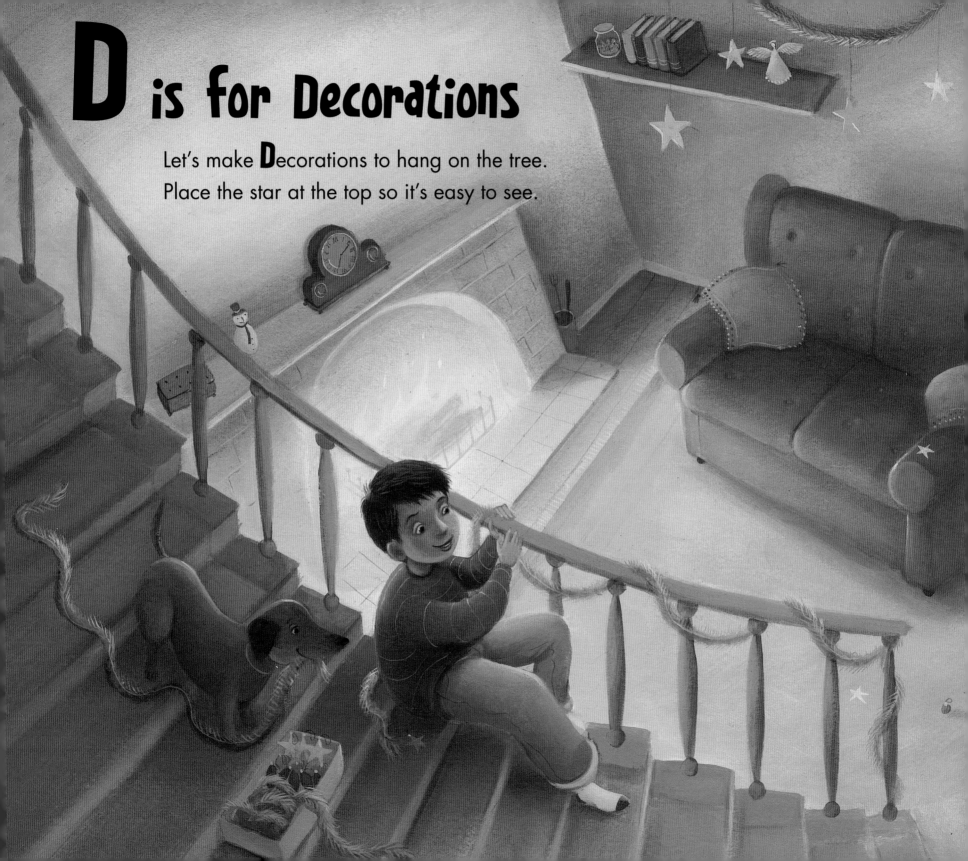

D is for Decorations

Let's make **D**ecorations to hang on the tree.
Place the star at the top so it's easy to see.

E is for Evergreen

The Evergreen branches
will twinkle with light
to tell us God's love is
eternally bright.

F is for Frost

God casts the **F**rost sparkling white on the land,
a beautiful blanket spread right from his hand.

G is for Gifts

It's time to share **G**ifts! God helps us believe
that **G**ifts are much better to give than receive.

Would you like **H**ot chocolate?
It's tasty and sweet.
Let's add the marshmallows—
Oh! What a treat.

H is for Hot chocolate

I is for Ice Skating

Winter means **I**ce skating; we love the sound
of our skates on the ice as we all spin around.

J is for Jingle bells

Jingle bells Jingle! The whole
world enjoys
the sound of bright bells as they
make joyful noise!

K is for Kind

In winter, be **K**ind doing chores great and small,
for we are God's workers and he loves us all!

L is for Lights

Winter means windows with Lights shining through.
Each candle reminds us that God's love is true.

M is for Mittens

Let's find our **M**ittens—we each have a pair,
and if we have extras we're happy to share!

N is for North wind

The North wind brings chills to our heads and our toes.
It sends the snow drifting wherever it blows.

O is for Overcoat

Put on your **O**vercoat—no time to fuss!
Warm coats are reminders that God protects us.

P is for Prayer

When walking outside in the cold icy air,
the silence of winter is perfect for **P**rayer.

Q is for Quilt

A Quilt on our laps as we sit down to rest,
each square tells a story of how we are blessed.

R is for Ride

It's time for a **R**ide on a
long wooden sled.
We race the others—now look
who's ahead!

S is for Snowman

Let's build a **S**nowman with eyes made of coal.
A top hat and scarf warm his jolly old soul!

T is for Trees

The Trees are all covered in snow pure and white,
a symbol of God's purest love and delight.

U is for Universe

In winter the **U**niverse calls us to play,
as beautiful nature surrounds us each day.

V is for Visit

A good time to Visit our friends young and old
and bring them hot soup when the weather is cold.

W is for Wonder

For winter brings **W**onder in things great and small,
and we must remember that God makes it all!

X is for eXtra-warm

The e**X**tra-warm blankets are stacked in a pile,
so let's go inside to warm up for a while.

Y is for Yarn

Knitting with Yarn as we sit side by side,
we look out the window and watch others slide.

Z is for Zoom

Zoom! goes a sled as it speeds down the hill.
God's love is warmth for a winter's day chill.

From mittens to snowmen and angels with wings—
may your hearts know the wonders that God's winter brings.